P9-ELR-714

Tow Truck Trouble

Adapted by Frank Berrios

Based on a story by Chuck Wilson

Illustrated by Dan Gracey, Andrew Phillipson,
and the Disney Storybook Artists

Random House 🏠 New York

Materials and characters from the movie *Cars*. Copyright © 2006, 2010 Disney/Pixar. Disney/Pixar elements © Disney/Pixar, not including underlying vehicles owned by third parties. Background inspired by the Cadillac Ranch by Ant Farm (Lord, Michels and Marquez) © 1974. All rights reserved. Published in the United States by Random House Children's Books, a division of Random House, Inc., 1745 Broadway, New York, NY 10019, and in Canada by Random House of Canada Limited, Toronto, in conjunction with Disney Enterprises, Inc. Random House and the colophon are registered trademarks of Random House, Inc.

Library of Congress Control Number: 2009939940   ISBN: 978-0-7364-2713-5

www.randomhouse.com/kids   MANUFACTURED IN CHINA   10 9 8 7 6 5

Mater's Rust Bucket Stadium wasn't very fancy, but there was always lots going on there. Mater hosted everything from car-jumping to tire-catching contests and loved to show off his tire-snagging skills.

One day, a big, mean tow truck named Bubba rolled into the stadium. Bubba was there with his pals, Tater and Tater Jr., to start trouble.

"Hey, Mater," said Bubba, "I challenge you to a racing derby—and the winner gets Rust Bucket Stadium!"

"Okay," replied Mater. He wasn't scared of a big bully like Bubba! The tow trucks agreed to compete in three events: tire-snagging, cone-dodging, and a one-lap all-out race to the finish line. The winner would own Rust Bucket Stadium.

Mater even agreed to let Tater and Tater Jr.
be the judges for the contest!
    Lightning McQueen thought Mater was crazy,
but he cheered his friend on anyway.

Tire-snagging was the first event. Guido threw a stack of tires into the air, and the tow trucks used their cables to hook as many of them as they could. Mater and Bubba snagged four tires each—but then Bubba knocked a tire off Mater's cable!

"Whoo-hoo, I win!" shouted Bubba.

The next event was cone-dodging. Mater and Bubba raced onto the track and zoomed around the turns. They kicked up lots of dust, but when the clouds settled, everyone saw that Mater had won! No one was better at cone-dodging than Mater.

Bubba just growled.

Mater and Bubba rolled up to the starting line for the last race, which would determine the big winner.

Bubba quickly took the lead. He dragged his tow hook back and forth behind him so Mater couldn't get in front. But at the final turn, Bubba's hook got caught in the track—and he flipped over!

Mater screeched to a stop. "Hold on, Bubba!" he said as he turned around.

Mater hooked his tow cable and pulled Bubba with all his might. But the tow truck was too heavy!

"Taters! I need Taters!" yelled Mater. "Bubba's in trouble, and we gotta help him."

So Tater and Tater Jr. used their cables to help Mater pull Bubba back up onto his wheels.

Bubba was so embarrassed that he sputtered out of the stadium without a word. The crowd cheered for Mater—the Rust Bucket Champion! Tater and Tater Jr. even asked him to teach them a few of his tricks.

"Sure thing," replied Mater. And he taught them how to snag tires—Mater style!

"Lightning," said a reporter back at the stadium, "do you have any words of wisdom for Chick and Stinger?"

"Yeah," said Lightning. "Racing the *wrong* way is never the *right* thing to do!"

The crowd cheered as Lightning crossed the finish line. Ramone and Lightning posed for photos with fans before accepting their Silver Tailfin trophy.

Stinger wasn't happy. He tried to take a shortcut through a parking garage. But he was going so fast, he didn't notice the warning sign for tire spikes.

Stinger heard all four of his tires pop, and he slowly came to a stop.

"Oh, no," he groaned as Lightning rolled past.

DO NOT ENTER

SEVERE
TIRE
DAMAGE!

As he roared out of the tunnel, Lightning heard
Stinger right behind him. Stinger poured on the speed
and slammed into Lightning as hard as he could.
Lightning never saw the big pothole in front of him—
but thanks to Stinger, he flew right over it.

"See you at the finish line!" Lightning said.

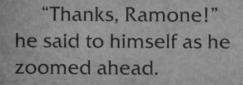

"Thanks, Ramone!"
he said to himself as he
zoomed ahead.

"Get ready to roll, Lightning!" yelled Ramone as he tagged his partner.

"You got it, buddy!" replied Lightning as he sped into the tunnel that started the second leg of the race.

Suddenly, the lights in the tunnel went out! Chick had turned them off, thinking that no one could race in the dark. But Lightning was glowing just enough to see where he was going.

That night, the crowd roared as Ramone and Chick made
their way to the starting line for the first leg of the race.

At the wave of the flag, the two cars took off! Chick tried
to cheat by pushing Ramone into a brick wall, but Ramone
was ready. He used his hydraulics to bounce over Chick at
the very last second—and watched as Chick smashed into
the wall!

Meanwhile, Chick Hicks was giving Stinger some last-minute tips. "Remember, stay in the lead," said Chick, "but if Lightning gets in front of you, use your bumper to push him out of your way."

"No problem," replied Stinger as he smashed into a pile of tires to show Chick he was ready. "Lightning won't know what hit him when he feels my sting."

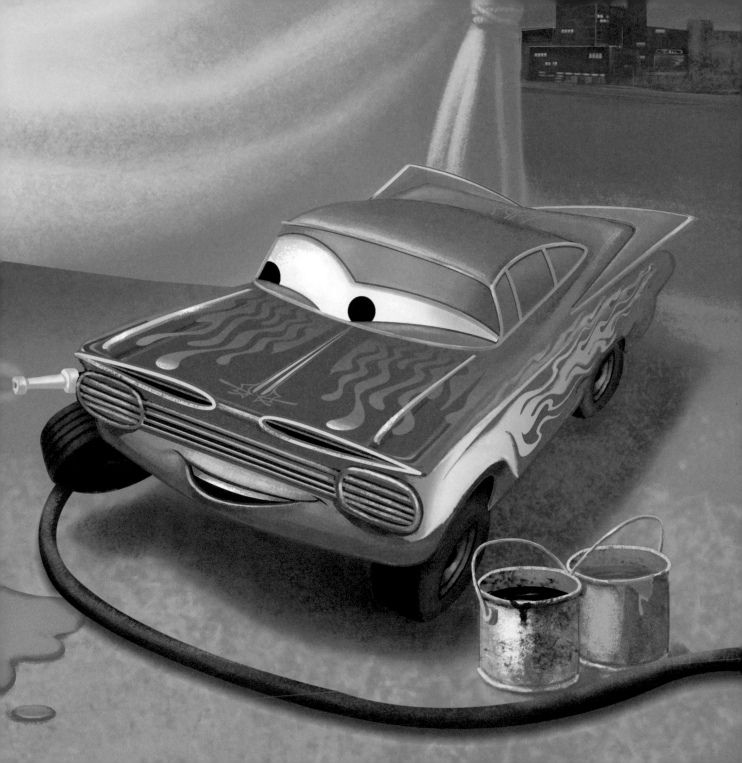

Ramone was so inspired by the neon lights that he decided to give Lightning McQueen a glow-in-the-dark paint job! Now everyone would be able to see Lightning—day or night!

Lightning McQueen and Ramone were excited when they arrived in Motoropolis City for the relay race against Chick Hicks and his racing school student, Stinger. Lightning was sporting some racing upgrades that gave him a cool new look! As they rolled down the street, both cars were enjoying the bright lights of the big city.

DISNEY · PIXAR

Cars

Lights Out!

Adapted by Frank Berrios

Based on a story by Lisa Marsoli

Illustrated by Dave Boelke, Jason Peltz, Andrew Phillipson,
and the Disney Storybook Artists

Random House 🏠 New York

Materials and characters from the movie *Cars*. Copyright © 2006, 2010 Disney/Pixar. Disney/Pixar elements © Disney/Pixar, not including underlying vehicles owned by third parties. Chevrolet Impala is a trademark of General Motors. All rights reserved. Published in the United States by Random House Children's Books, a division of Random House, Inc., 1745 Broadway, New York, NY 10019, and in Canada by Random House of Canada Limited, Toronto, in conjunction with Disney Enterprises, Inc., Random House and the colophon are registered trademarks of Random House, Inc.
Library of Congress Control Number: 2009939940
www.randomhouse.com/kids   MANUFACTURED IN CHINA
ISBN: 978-0-7364-2713-5
1 0 9 8 7 6 5